George Washburn Smalley

A review of Mr. Bright's speeches

George Washburn Smalley

A review of Mr. Bright's speeches

ISBN/EAN: 9783337173807

Printed in Europe, USA, Canada, Australia, Japan

Cover: Foto ©Andreas Hilbeck / pixelio.de

More available books at **www.hansebooks.com**

A REVIEW

OF

MR. BRIGHT'S SPEECHES.

A REVIEW

OF

MR. BRIGHT'S SPEECHES.

BY

GEORGE WASHBURN SMALLEY.

REPRINTED FROM THE "NEW YORK TRIBUNE."

London:

MACMILLAN AND CO.

1868.

LONDON :

R. CLAY, SONS, AND TAYLOR, PRINTERS,
BREAD STREET HILL.

A REVIEW

OF

MR. BRIGHT'S SPEECHES.*

EXCEPTING those who have been fortunate enough to hear Mr. Bright in England, few Americans have an accurate or complete notion of his powers as an orator. They know him by reputation and by imperfect reports of some of his speeches printed in fine type in the New York journals. Naturally, also, most of the speeches republished in this country have been those on American topics, or on Reform, a subject of scarcely less interest here than in England. It is possible now to get a better notion of the scope of Mr. Bright's genius. The two handsome and clearly printed volumes published in

* Speeches on Questions of Public Policy. By John Brigh M.P. Edited by James E. Thorold Rogers. Two Vols. 8 London : Macmillan & Co.

London by Mr. Macmillan include speeches on nearly
every important topic which during the last quarter
of a century has enlisted the attention of England.
The selection and editing of them was assigned to
Professor Thorold Rogers, lately Professor of Political
Economy at Oxford, now ejected from his chair
because of his Liberalism.   His task demanded a good
knowledge of politics, exact culture, and not a little
common sense.   It has been well done.   Mr. Bright
himself has revised the text, and, on the whole, the
book offers us such a record of a great career, and
such a monument of eloquence as few orators, ancient
or modern, have been able to give to the world.

Mr. Rogers has wisely arranged these speeches in
groups.   A chronological order might have been con-
venient to the professional student of oratory, but
the general reader, and the student who consults them
as a repertory of political information and instruction,
will be thankful to find the speeches under their
proper heads.   There are five speeches on India,
three on Canada, seven on America, nine on Ireland,
four on Russia, and thirteen on Reform.   The enume-
ration of these leading topics is enough to show the
great range which the orations take.   There are, in
addition, fifteen single speeches on fifteen other sub-

jects, including Free Trade, Land, Peace, Foreign and
Financial Policy, the Punishment of Death, Education,
and matters of the like highest social and political
importance. The earliest speeches given were made
in 1845; much the greatest number belong to the
last fifteen years; many of the greatest orations to
the last three years.

Like Wordsworth's Prelude, these volumes are the
history of the growth of a man's mind. Few men
are born orators, few first speeches succeed. Mr.
Bright is no exception to the rule. Nothing in his
speeches is more instructive to the student than the
contrast between his earlier and later manner; between, for instance, two speeches which are placed
together by accident in the first volume. Both
relate to Ireland. One was delivered in 1849, the
other in 1866. One is the work of an artist whose
genius struggles with an imperfect command of his
tools; the other is the perfect utterance of a mature
mind, still kindling with the inspiration of youth, and
enriched with all the resources of a difficult art that
has been thoroughly mastered. We believe there is
no tradition that Mr. Bright needed to use pebbles,
like Demosthenes, to improve his articulation. That
was the smallest part of the labours which the Greek

orator endured. It needs only to read these speeches critically to see that prodigious toil has been spent on attaining the excellence which they now display. The diction is such as came never to any man by inspiration ; it is the fruit of incessant practice. Rochdale has a churchyard overlooking the town, chiefly famous as being the burial-place of "Tim Bobbin," a quaint Lancashire poet of much local fame. There are men living who remember Mr. Bright, then a very young man, taking his stand by Tim Bobbin's grave, making speeches to a public meeting assembled in the churchyard to protest against the compulsory collection of church-rates. It was his first lesson, and they say the speech was poor enough, read from the manuscript into the bargain.* Some years later, when the agitation against the Corn Laws began, Mr. Bright resolved to make an experiment as lecturer. He was then on a visit to his friend Mr. Thomasson, of Bolton. The experiment was tried before a Mechanics' Institute, and, like Mr. Disraeli, upon his first essay in the House, Mr. Bright broke down, and his friend Mr. Poulson finished the lecture for him.

---

* This, I am told, is a mistake. Mr. Bright, says my informant, who ought to know, never read a speech on any question of public policy.

He was not the man to be disheartened, and before many years he was speaking night after night by the side of Mr. Cobden to the immense audiences which in those days crowded Covent Garden Theatre in London, and the largest halls of the provincial towns. He was a popular speaker; an orator he had not become. We have turned over the volumes of *The League*, the newspaper published by the Corn Law agitators, in which numbers of his early speeches are reported at length. There is not much promise in them. Some qualities which go to the making of good speeches are there—boldness, exact knowledge, passion, profound conviction. There is invective enough, but it is commonplace; vehement, but not forcible. His style was diffuse; it had neither richness of diction, nor imaginative power. Those who heard him, say that his voice was then his best oratorical endowment. It was and is a very noble instrument, of great compass and easily under command. Its volume compelled a certain deliberation of utterance which was an advantage to a young speaker. He had time to choose his words, and in time his vocabulary grew copious. In 1843, speaking in Covent Garden, and bent on saying his worst of the Lords, he could only describe them as a " miser-

able aristocracy." Nobody was much hurt by that.
Twenty-two years later, in Birmingham Town Hall,
he pictured the foreign policy and wars of England,
based on the balance of power theory, as "a gigantic
system of out-door relief for the aristocracy of Great
Britain." System and aristocracy together shook
under such a satire. There is no finer example of his
best manner.

It was Pitt, if we remember rightly, who was said
to be familiar with no English poet but Spenser, to
which it was replied that he who knew Spenser well
had a good hold upon the English tongue. Dryden
was the favourite of Fox, and his remark is well
known that he would use no word not to be found in
that author. Mr. Bright has made Milton his study.
Probably the only Englishman who knew Milton
equally well was Macaulay, who declared that, if
every copy of Paradise Lost were destroyed, he believed he could reproduce the poem from his memory.
Mr. Bright is said by his friends to have all the
poems, or nearly all, by heart. We imagine that he
has also wrought deeply in a mine too little explored
by most students — the prose works of the same
author. There are many passages in these orations
which have the grandeur of Milton's manner, in

whom the classical and scriptural influences were singularly blended. There is daring imagery, passionate force, sustained magnificence of diction in many of the perorations. To some criticism on his want of acquaintance with the classical languages of antiquity, it was well replied that he knows English as Demosthenes knew Greek.

Mr. Bright always speaks from notes. The question of what is called extempore speaking need never be raised in respect to any great orator. There never was an orator who spoke without preparation. The preparation is sometimes for a particular speech, sometimes the study and practice of a score of years blossom out in what is called an impromptu oration; but no great speech ever was impromptu. His popular addresses are made from notes on slips of paper. In the House of Commons he appears to use small tablets of card, each topic being on a separate slip, and the slips being thus capable of rearrangement as the debate proceeds. The " justification " of these tablets, to use a printer's phrase, is often observed by the House as the first indication that he means to enter the debate. There are other signs. One night, during the last session, many inquiries were made in the lobbies whether Mr. Bright intended to speak.

"No," said a member who knew him well; "Mr. Bright is making all sorts of sallies and repartees in the smoking room. He never does that when he is going to address the House." Before he rises he is pre-occupied in manner, answers questions briefly, and wastes no strength on side topics.

He had not been long in Parliament before he became noted as a speaker. As the phrase is, he got the ear of the House. Then, and ever since, when the cry was heard, "Bright is up!" the telegraph wires flashed the news to the clubs, members came rushing down in cabs, the dining and smoking rooms were deserted, the Peers came over to the Commons, the strangers' galleries were always crowded. Friends and enemies were equally eager to hear him. His three years' illness, and his absence from Parliament after his rejection by Manchester in 1855, in consequence of his opposition to the Crimean war, proved of great benefit to the orator. He had had twenty years' practice. He added to it the strength which comes from repose and reflection. His oratory gained in stateliness of style, in richness of humour, and in compression. All his subsequent speeches are cast in one mould. They have a classical severity of form, which is preserved without change, yet without monotony. Lord Brougham said that every perfect oration must be partly written and partly extemporised from the moment. He carried his theory so far that you can see the joints in his speeches.' Mr. Bright evidently prepares his perorations—no speech is without one ; but they flow naturally out of the subject. The orator rises by degrees that are imperceptible, and the effect is never impaired by an appearance of intention. This is true of all the great speeches since 1858 ; true of none before that date.

Few men have taken such liberties with the House as Mr. Bright has. It is a body impatient of oratory ; he has taught it to listen with respect and admiration to his highest flights. It dislikes earnestness and despises enthusiasm, but tolerates and applauds both when Mr. Bright is on his feet. Pathos, the unchecked expression of natural emotions, are reckoned as much out of place in the Commons as at a dinner-table ; but nothing seems out of place when Mr. Bright is the speaker. Lord Halifax, then Sir Charles Wood, said many years ago that Mr. Bright was the first debater in the House—of which Sir Charles Wood, a dull man, was a good judge—and that he was much more ; that he had used figures of speech which no other orator in modern times could have ventured

upon. He might almost have thrown Burke's dagger
on the floor. In the speech of December 24, 1854,
when the British army lay starving and freezing in
the stupid trenches before Sebastopol, he sought to
impress the House with a sense of the reality of the
losses they were suffering ; how they came home to
the firesides and hearts of men ; and how the Ministry
was responsible for all. The passage is indescribably
touching, and is a good instance of the employment
of details to give life to a picture :—

"We all know what we have lost in this House. Here,
sitting near me, very often sat the Member for Frome
(Colonel Boyle). I met him a short time before he went
out, at Mr. Westerton's, the bookseller, near Hyde Park
Corner. I asked him whether he was going out. He
answered, he was afraid he was ; not afraid in the sense of
personal fear—he knew not that—but he said with a look
and a tone I shall never forget, 'It is no light matter for a
man who has a wife and five little children.' The stormy
Euxine is his grave ; his wife is a widow, his children
fatherless."

The conclusion of the speech in which this passage
occurs may be quoted as an example of the height to
which the orator rises in concluding a great oration,
and of his unsparing condemnation of the war and
those who were responsible for it :—

" I am not, nor did I ever pretend to be, a statesman ; and that character is so tainted and equivocal in our day, that I am not sure that a pure and honourable ambition would aspire to it. I have not enjoyed for thirty years, like these noble lords, the honours and emoluments of office. I have not set my sails to every passing breeze. I am a plain and simple citizen, sent here by one of the foremost constituencies of the Empire, representing feebly perhaps, but honestly I dare aver, the opinions of very many, and the true interests of all those who have sent me here. Let it not be said that I am alone in my condemnation of this war and of this incapable and guilty Administration. And even if I were alone, if mine were a solitary voice raised amid the din of arms and the clamours of a venal press, I should have the consolation I have to-night—and which I trust will be mine to the last moment of my existence—the priceless consolation that no word of mine has tended to promote the squandering of my country's treasure, or the spilling of one single drop of my country's blood."

It is not easy to find one among living orators between whom and Mr. Bright there is much resemblance. A number of men have great fame as public speakers, both in England and America. Among the English, Lord Derby probably deserves to be first mentioned. The success of his public career has been due to his oratory more than to any other personal quality—more than to anything but his rank and wealth, which gave him a natural leadership of the aristocracy. Mr. Bright said in 1866 that the accession to office of Lord Derby was a declaration of war against the working classes. Still more vehemently, in November of the same year, he described him as a man who had never shown one atom of statesmanship, or one spark of patriotism. And Lord Derby described himself as a man whose mission it was to stem democracy. Such a man could never be a popular orator. He has been the orator of good society, and conferred a signal benefit upon the House of Lords by importing into that rather sleepy conclave a vivacious element. He early got the name of the "Rupert of Debate," and long deserved it— deserves it even now, in his seventieth year. In speech, as in action, he was fiery and rash. The impetuous cavalry leader of the Cavaliers was not more so. But he is never in a vulgar haste. His speech is patrician. He delights in ornate sentences, abounds in classical allusions, and pleases himself by taking it for granted that all his hearers know Greek.

Lord Russell never won fame as an orator. He is a good debater, understands the House as well as any man, and knows how to say a severe thing. A scorn of opponents that is even ill-bred, a strong, clear, narrow way of putting things, and a talent for irony, are his chief characteristics as a speaker. But orator he is not.

Mr. Cobden's name is associated imperishably with Mr. Bright's. They had much in common as states- men, not much as orators. Mr. Cobden was an effective speaker, but never a great orator. He had vigour without art. His power lay in freshness of thought and originality of illustration; above all, in practical knowledge of his subject. He spoke as an authority. He cared more for substance than form. His addresses always had a conversational tone, which Mr. Bright's never have. The deliberation of his style was excessive, and could not have kept the attention of an audience not thoroughly interested both in the speaker and his subject. But his self-possession was supreme. He held his ideas, as it were, in solution. They floated visibly before him, and came and went at his bidding. He had a habit of qualifying phrases, and re-stating doctrines, until he arrived at the exact point which he wished to impress upon his hearers. His speeches were never complete, while Mr. Bright's always had a definite form in his own mind before they were uttered.

One of the men who in a few years more would

have been the leader of the Tory party in the House
of Commons, has been translated to the Upper House.
Lord Cranborne was a power below the gangway.
His speech was compact, energetic, and impassioned.
Nobody could say harder things in fewer words,
and he poured out the vials of an unmeasured contempt on the Ministry from which he had withdrawn.
There is no match for him in the Lords, where he now
sits as Marquis of Salisbury.

There are four or five speakers who are masters
of the conversational style of debate which is valued
and effective in the House. Mr. Roebuck projects
angry sarcasms with immense force. He is always
disliked, but always listened to. Mr. Lowe distils
epigrams with the most perfectly nonchalant air, is
as full of facts as Macaulay, and as sparkling as
Sheridan, perfectly good-humoured, perfectly unscru-
pulous, and one of the most dangerous opponents a
Minister or a measure ever has to confront. Mr.
Mill's success has not been due to any display of
oratorical power. Mr. Coleridge, who will be Attor-
ney-General in the next Government, has a persuasive
and flowing speech, very unusual with an Englishman and very popular with the House. Mr. Bright
said recently, at Exeter, that he scarcely ever heard

a more beautiful speech than that delivered by Mr. Coleridge in the last Irish debate—and beautiful was just the word. Mr. Disraeli is the best example of that style of debate which Lord Palmerston practised. The gravest subjects are discussed in the jauntiest tone. For every occasion there is one fundamental maxim—the House is to be amused, must not be bored, and is to be kept in good humour with itself and with the speaker. It always enjoys personalities, and Mr. Disraeli never makes a speech without them. But Mr. Disraeli's imitation of Lord Palmerston is at most an imitation of manner, and for every good-humoured jest with which the one amused the House, his successor has a biting sneer. The House is a critic of style, and will stand any amount of windy generalization if the diction be neat. An assertion that would be too strong if put forward nakedly, will bring down cheers when embroidered with a felicitous rhetorical conceit. In all these arts, and many more, Mr. Disraeli is expert. The employment of them all in a speech produces something that is very curious, and often admirable, considered as a means to an end ; but it does not present Mr. Disraeli as a rival in oratory to Mr. Bright. Clinging to the high sense of that word, there is after all no one but Mr. Gladstone who can contest his supremacy. Mr. Gladstone has one quality too much for a perfect orator. His mind is subtle in excess. He delights in refinements. He seldom makes the broad, simple, unqualified statement which alone reaches and convinces a popular audience. The involution of his sentences would drive an uncultivated hearer to despair. There is curious skill in his management of a series of clauses and parentheses, and qualifications and explanations which take their winding way from one end of a sentence to the other. They are effective if the audience has a logical training as severe as that of the speaker, but they are confusing and at last wearisome to plain people who look for a verb to follow its nominative at a reasonable distance. No grace is wanting to Mr. Gladstone's speech that culture can give. He knows many languages, yet he does not know English so well as Mr. Bright. More than all, his sympathy with an audience is far less complete than Mr. Bright's, and his mind does not work on a level with those he addresses. He is best in the House, and the best proof of his great power is, that though every speech is pervaded with the earnestness of intense conviction, and though the House hates nothing so much as that a man should be in earnest, it listens always, and often suffers itself to be swayed and carried over by the orator whom it more than half dislikes. Of Mr. Bright the same is true. When he was in a minority almost of one, when he attacked the idols of the House, when he resisted its wishes, and even when he stemmed for a moment the irresistible current of such a passion as that which possessed England during the Crimean War, he always extorted attention and admiration.

In America, the number of clever speakers is greater than in England, but it is still difficult to find one who bears a close likeness to Mr. Bright. We have graceful lecturers like Curtis, actors like Gough, one great pulpit orator in Beecher, who can turn the platform into a pulpit, and the pulpit into a platform, and work miracles of human speech on either. We have men fluent and powerful on the stump, like Frederick Douglass, and campaign speakers of tireless activity, like Henry Wilson. Nobody will doubt that we abound in advocates at the Bar of great persuasive talent, purely intellectual, like Dana of Boston and O'Conor; plausible, like Evarts, or filled with natural fire, as was Andrew, whom we have lately lost. Ready debaters we do not lack, skilled in parliamentary warfare, with a conscience, like Boutwell, or without, like Fessenden. And the Senate can boast of one speaker perfect in rhetorical art, of the broadest culture, and of a faith and courage that long since made Charles Sumner's a shining name among American statesmen and orators. Some years ago there was a public man whose speeches we admired as eloquent defences of morals in politics, but the Seward who announced at Rochester the irrepressible conflict, and whose voice swept free over the prairies in 1856, is dead. Of all these men and their many compeers, there is no one who can be described as an orator in the sense in which we use that word of Demosthenes, of Mirabeau, of Chatham, of Patrick Henry, of O'Connell, of Henry Clay, of John Bright, and among living Americans, of Wendell Phillips alone.

Among Americans recently dead, Webster was nearest to Bright in what we may call the merely external characteristics of oratory. Mr. Bright lacks the imposing stature of Webster, which, combined with the colossal mould of his features and limbs, almost entitled him to the epithet majestic, by which adoring Boston delighted to describe him. The traits of actual resemblance between the two are slight, yet to an American who sees Bright for the first time on the platform, the memory of Webster will be sure to return. What the two had in common was the power to produce on the mind the sensation of massiveness. There are other marks of likeness, a slow delivery, an elocution sustained and stately—both sovereigns over the audiences they addressed. Webster in Faneuil Hall, Bright in the Free Trade Hall at Manchester, alike bore sway, and the minds of men became obedient to their will before it was uttered. Theodore Parker said of Webster, " He could state a case better than any man in America." The same power belongs to Bright. But the remark was not only true of Webster, it was almost exhaustive, and it does not begin to be exhaustive when applied to the English orator. The intellectual forces of Webster were all summed up in the word understanding. Imagination he lacked. Pathos he despised—unless at an advanced period after dinner. Passion was not his, nor that force without which all other force is weak, and which is to be found only in strength of conviction, and absolute loyalty to the law of conscience. Webster no more believed in the existence of such a thing as principle than Thurlow Weed. The two agreed in regarding it as an imaginary motive by which persons professed to be guided in some actions which could not be intelligibly explained on the ordinary grounds of self-interest. There were certain terms, such as conscience, morality, law of God, which Webster recognised as having a rhetorical value, and he employed them as he often did Biblical illustrations. He had the same opinion about them as a Roman augur had about the entrails of a chicken, or an Indian medicine-man about the charms by which he invoked rain and averted pestilence. They imposed on the people, and they were a source of profit to the impostor who used them. It was rank heresy once to confess so much as this in respect to Webster. Nobody ever thought or ever will think of casting such imputations on John Bright. He has been attacked often, and on many grounds, but it has not occurred to his enemies to suspect him of insincerity. It is easy to differ from Mr. Bright, but it is impossible to hear him, or even to read his printed speech, and doubt that every word is genuine. And we are clearly of opinion that to an orator there is no single quality, no sum of qualities, so essential to his success as sincerity. If you wish to persuade others, first be persuaded yourself.

That is the first mark of similarity between Bright and Wendell Phillips—a profound sincerity of character. Mr. Bright is a Quaker, clinging faithfully to the best traditions of that people. Mr. Phillips is a Puritan, tracing his ancestry through six generations of New England ministers, the truest representatives of the true Puritan stock. Both have won fame by a life-long devotion to reforms. Both early learned to believe in something, which is on the whole the best lesson ever learned in this world, and the basis of every great speech that ever was made. The careers of the two men have been very different. Mr. Phillips was born to wealth and social position, educated in the best culture America could give, and every avenue to professional or political distinction and office lay wide open before him. He turned aside from all to devote his genius to one unpopular cause. Abolition owed much to the zeal of its earlier advocates, but for many years before the war it had become so odious and so weak, that it needed the eloquence and political sagacity of Phillips to rescue it from popular contempt and even from oblivion. During the Corn Law agitation which brought Mr. Bright into public life, he always had on his side great commercial interests, unlimited funds, and a powerful political machinery. Mr. Phillips fought his battle for twenty-five years, not only without aid from such sources, but with every one of them arrayed

against him.   He spoke often at the peril of his life.
It was a sterner school than that which the Englishman passed through, and its influence on the American
orator is perceptible in every speech.   To persuade
an audience of men whose convictions and interests
are doubtful or opposed to you, but who come to hear
you, is one thing.   To confront a mob who come to
silence you and to succeed in silencing them, is quite
another.   The condensation, vigour, and point which
characterise Mr. Phillips's speeches could alone have
caught the ear of the rioting audiences of the years
before the war.   Against such audiences the polished
invective which Mr. Phillips employs with such merci-
less force was a weapon of self-defence.   He has been
heard on the lecture-platform by large numbers of
Americans, but his greatest speeches were delivered
elsewhere than in lyceums; many of them to the
mobs; many of them before legislative committees,
equally hostile but more orderly.   There is no speaker
either in England or America who can be compared
with Phillips in grace and elegance, whether of
appearance, manner, or diction.   His oratory has a
magical quality, a charm that wins every audience, but
is indescribable, a force and splendour which partly
explain the immense influence on the popular mind

exercised for many years by this almost solitary champion of a hated cause.

Mr. Bright has contrived to carry on business and politics together during all his life, making at the same time excellent cotton goods, and the best speeches in England. If orators may be divided into the philosophical and the practical, he clearly belongs to the practical. He has an immense fund of common sense. There are imaginative passages in his orations, but in his loftiest flights the ground is still firm under his feet. He delights in details, and in bringing to bear upon politics the experience he has gained in the counting-house and the mill. He is English in every fibre, with the English contempt for generalization. There is seldom any reach of thought in his speeches that could be called speculative, and nothing that approaches the metaphysical. The principles to which he always recurs are moral or political. No danger of his wearying the House, like Burke, by refining while they thought of dining. His oratorical triumphs have been gained in dealing with practical questions. His fame as orator and his fame as statesman are so intertwined that one can scarcely be separated from the other. Free Trade was the most practical of questions, it touched the pocket, and almost nothing

else. India was another ; ameliorate its government,
was his demand, in order that you may encourage the
growth of cotton. War, and the Crimean War in
particular, he denounced as an injury to trade, and the
commercial argument was put forward so prominently
as to give rise to Lord Palmerston's sarcasm that if
the enemy were to land on the shores of England, Mr.
Bright would make a calculation whether it would be
cheaper to take him in or keep him out. But Mr.
Bright's hatred of war rested on other and higher
grounds. When we come to such questions as Ireland,
America, and Reform, the better qualities of the
orator's intellect display themselves. It is no longer
the necessities of trade or the protection of property ;
trade and property would have been much obliged to
Mr. Bright if he would have left these three topics
untouched. Trade thought it had nothing to do with
equal rights, and heard with fear the cry, Be just to
the Irish, give America fair play and the sympathies
due to a people contending for freedom, and give the
people of England control of the government of
England. On Reform he is almost the first English
statesman who demonstrated that the franchise was a
right, and not a privilege to be grudgingly conceded
by some superior power. The noblest passages in

these orations, some of the noblest in any language, are those which relate to these highest political themes.

The familiar paradox, " Does it read well ? Then it was not a good speech," must do duty once more for the sake of being refuted. Mr. Bright's speeches were good when they were made, and they are good to read. They are not only interesting, instructive, and eloquent, they are often amusing. There are few speeches in the two volumes which are not enlivened by touches of a rare humour. Mr. Bright likes fun, knows the value of a good story in relieving the strained attention of an audience, and knows how to tell it. He has an exquisite talent for unexpected hits in the middle of a sentence. The value of suddenness as an element of wit is a thing he understands. The House of Peers is feathered all over with the shafts he has left sticking in its members. " Their families find employment—at least they find salaries—in the military or naval service." Legislation is better since than before the Reform Bill, but it is ' owing chiefly to the general intelligence of the people —" an intelligence which has penetrated *even into* the House of Commons and into the House of Lords." The law dare not *say* that game is property, and

cannot say so, but " we have several Acts of Parliament, clauses of the utmost complication, traps of
every kind, as many to catch the poacher as the
poacher has to catch the game." The passage on
Americanising England is too long to quote, but is
brimful of fun, and as witty as Sydney Smith's
taxation caricature. If he wants to describe a
flunkey, he finds means to do it without using that
objectionable word at all ; certain persons whom he
does not like are " men who, if they were dressed in
the garb that most becomes them, would be dressed
in plush." He does not disdain the homeliest illustration. Speaking in the House of Commons—which
is critical in such matters—during the Russian War,
he said of the Vienna Conferences :

" Well, Sir, the terms offered are called 'bases,' from which
one understands, not that they are everything, but that they
are something capable of what diplomatists call 'development.' I recollect a question asked of a child at school in
one of those lessons called 'object lessons,' 'What is the
basis of batter pudding?' It was obvious that flour was the
basis ; but the eggs and the butter and the rest were deve-
lopments and additions. But, if the bases are capable of
development, so I take it for granted that the meaning of
negotiation is not the offering of an *ultimatum*, but the word
involves to every man's sense the probability of concession—
butter, it may be—but concession of one sort or another.'

Nor did he shrink from attacking even the newspapers, any more than we shrink from quoting what
he said because it sometimes bore hard on the habits
of our profession. There was an alarm in England
in 1865 on the subject of Canada, which Mr. Bright
thought ridiculous. " It is said the newspapers have
got into a panic. They can do that any night between
the hours of six and twelve o'clock, when they write
their articles." In a speech on the American War
in 1863, he quoted Jefferson's somewhat impertinent
remark that "newspapers should be divided into four
compartments : in one of them they should print the
true ; in the next, the probable ; in the third, the
possible ; and in the fourth, the lies.' " With regard
to some of these newspapers," said Mr. Bright—and,
remembering what some of them were at that time in
England, we can appreciate the force of his opinion
—" I incline to think, as far as their leading columns
go, that an equal division of space would be found
very inconvenient, and that the last-named compart-
ment, when dealing with American questions, would
have to be at least four times as large as the first."
He did not keep all his expositions for the Tory
press, but described the *Spectator* with great truth
as " a paper which certainly is not very Radical—

is rather, in my opinion, though conducted with considerable ability, conceited in some of its criticisms upon us." As for the *Times*, there is more truth told about that journal in these volumes than can be found in any printed book that we know of excepting Kinglake's "Invasion of the Crimea." We have quoted some of the judgments in another part of this review. Americans will do well to keep in mind Mr. Bright's remark, that the *Times*, unfortunately and *untruly*, is believed to represent the opinions of the English people. It represents the Plutocracy, yet is far from understanding even their interests. When Mr. Cobden's French Treaty was made, "we had it commented on by a great journal in this country, whose motives I will not attempt to divine, but whose motto must, I think, be that which Pascal said ought to have been adopted by one of the ancients—' *Omnia pro tempore, sed nihil pro veritate*,'—which being translated may be rendered, ' Everything for the *Times*, but nothing for truth.' "

Personality is one of the many charges often brought against Mr. Bright. There are a few very famous examples of it, and all of them are to be found in these volumes. None of the speeches has been expurgated ; no speech omitted for fear of giving or renewing offence. After all, there is not much, and there is not any which does not appear to have been richly deserved or provoked. The reputation sprung not from the frequency, but from the severity, of the instances. The House of Commons is not exactly a school of good manners, and its politeness is so extremely parliamentary as sometimes to become Pickwickian. The ferocious hostilities which embittered the debates of the last century are not just now in vogue. The spirit may be the same, but its expression is more decorous, and there are known, though not very accurate, limits to the personal encounters which occur from time to time in that arena. The complaint of personality is mostly cant. There is not a politician of eminence at this moment living in Great Britain who has not in his time attacked his opponents on personal grounds—who has not resorted to the *ad hominem* argument when he found himself at a loss for others. Mr. Bright can hit tremendously hard, and, like most men conscious of great powers, uses them sparingly against inferiors. When his equals step into the ring, there is a good deal of give and take on both sides. Perhaps Mr. Bright could say with more truth than Mr. Disraeli recently did, that he never attacked anybody in his life, unless first assailed. Almost everybody at one time or another had assailed him. The celebrated onslaught on Lord Palmerston in 1861 grew out of the mutilation of the despatches of Sir Alexander Burnes on the Affghan War, which had been presented to Parliament so altered as to justify, whereas in fact they condemned, the policy of the Government. A Committee was moved for to ascertain who falsified the documents. There was no direct evidence who did it; but Mr. Bright charged it upon Lord Palmerston. "The noble lord," he exclaimed, "is on trial in this case. He attempted to say that what was left out was unimportant, but I should like to ask the noble lord what was the object of the minute and ingenious, and I will say unmatched care which was taken in mutilating the despatches of a gentleman whose opinions were of no importance, and whose writings could not make the slightest difference either to the question or to the opinions of any person concerned? The noble lord, too, has stooped to conduct which, if I were not in this House, I might describe in language which I could not possibly use here without being told that I was transgressing the line usually observed in discussions in this assembly." He dwelt with unforgiving reiteration on the charge : "It is admitted—and the noble lord has not flatly

denied it—he cannot deny it—he knows it as well as
the honourable and learned member for Greenock—
*he knows it as well as the very man whose hand did
the evil*—he knows there have been garbling, mutilation, practically and essentially falsehood and forgery
in those despatches which have been laid before the
House." And in the conclusion of his speech he exclaimed : " Once more I ask the noble lord to tell us
who did it. He knows who did it. Was it his own
right hand, or was it Lord Broughton's right hand, or
was it some clever Secretary in the Foreign Office, or
in the India Office, who did this work ? I say the
House has a right to know. We want to know *that*.
We want to drag the delinquent before the public.
This we want to know because we wish to deter other
Ministers from committing the like offence ; and we
want to know it for that which most of all is neces-
sary—to vindicate the character and honour of
Parliament." But the Committee was refused. Still
more famous, because more recent, is his humorous
account of the secession of Mr. Horsman and Mr.
Lowe from the Liberal party on the Reform Bill of
1866. No political nickname was ever more successful
than the Cave of Adullam. The first application of
it was in the following passage in Mr. Bright's speech

on the Russell Reform Bill in the House, March 13, 1866 :—

" The right honourable gentleman below me (Mr. Horsman) said a little against the Government, and a little against the bill, but had last night a field night for an attack upon so humble an individual as I am. The right honourable gentleman is the first of the new party who has expressed his great grief, who has retired into what may be called his political Cave of Adullam, and he has called about him every one that was in distress and every one that was discontented. The right honourable gentleman has been long anxious to form a party in this House. There is scarcely any one on this side of the House who is able to address the House with effect or take much part in our debates whom he has not tried to bring over to his party or cabal; and at last the right honourable gentleman has succeeded in hooking the right honourable gentleman the member for Calne (Mr. Lowe). I know there was an opinion expressed many years ago by a Member of the Treasury Bench and of the Cabinet, that two men would make a party. When a party is formed of two men so amiable, so discreet as the two right honourable gentlemen, we may hope to see for the first time in Parliament a party perfectly harmonious—and distinguished by mutual and unbroken trust. But there is one difficulty which it is impossible to remove. This party of two reminds me of the Scotch terrier, which was so covered with hair that you could not tell which was the head and which was the tail of it."

To relish this as the House relished it, the extreme

unpopularity and pugnacity of Messrs. Horsman and Lowe need to be borne in mind. Mr. Disraeli this year struck a similar vein in describing Mr. Lowe as possessing "a power of spontaneous aversion." In the same speech Mr. Bright went on to say :—

"The right honourable gentleman told us of the polypus, which takes its colour from the rock on which it lives, and he said that some honourable members take their colours from their constituencies. The constituency which the right honourable gentleman represents consists of 174 men, seven of whom are working-men; but the real constituency of the right honourable gentleman is a member of the other House of Parliament, and he could send in his butler or his groom, instead of the right honourable gentleman, to represent the borough. I think, in one sense—regarding the right honourable gentleman as an intellectual gladiator in this House—we are much indebted to the Marquis of Lansdowne that he did not do that."

If his satire is sometimes elaborate, it is also sometimes concise, and he has a way of transfixing his enemies with a phrase, as when he spoke of the "unsleeping ill-will" of Lord Cranborne toward America, or the "indiscriminating abuse" of Mr. Roebuck; and he photographed, in a parenthesis, the truculent member for Sheffield as one who had "managed to get rid of all those feelings under which all men, black and white, like to be free." The editor of the *Times*,

Mr. Delane, becomes "the Man in the Mask, endeavouring to stab me in the back." He has touched the difference between what such a man dare do with and without his mask, by quoting the description of Fernando Wood, who walked uprightly before the world, but when he was not before the world his walk was slantindicular. The *Times* itself he denounces often—is one of few men who have ventured to affront and attack it openly and have come off victorious. Cobden did, and Kinglake did. Mr. Bright expressed what he truly felt, a mixture of indignation and contempt :—

"No man laments more than I do that so much power should be associated with what I will call a godless intellect and a practical atheism. No one laments more than I do that a paper which was once great in its independence has become now—what shall I say?—domesticated; for the editor of *The Times* is now domesticated in the houses of Cabinet Ministers and members of high families in London. He has learned now—in this day, when that paper might have been more useful than ever—to fetch and carry for Cambridge House," (which then was the residence of Lord Palmerston).

Often his sarcasm takes the shape of jest, and he has great power of suggesting ludicrous images. Most men have found something to make fun of in

Earl Russell. The pomposity of the noble lord lays
him constantly open to the shafts of his opponents.
"He told us," said Mr. Bright in a speech during the
Crimean War, "that he still intended to leave Russia
a great empire. I thought that exceedingly conside-
rate of the noble lord, and I understand—I think it
has been stated in the public papers—that it is considered at St. Petersburg a great condescension on the
part of so eminent a statesman." And when in the
same year Mr. Roebuck brought forward a motion
which frightened Lord Russell into his desertion of
Lord Aberdeen, Mr. Bright transmitted to posterity
the picture of Mr. Roebuck "coming forward as a
little David with sling and stone, weapons which he
did not even use, but at the sight of which the Whig
Goliath went howling and vanquished to the back
benches." Good as this is, the fun is half lost in
quotation. It was irresistible in the House itself when
the orator launched his dart in person at this Whig
Goliath, five feet high, perched at the moment on a
seat from which his legs dangled half-way to the
floor.

He attacked classes more often than individuals,
and the abuse of power which had got lodged in the
citadel of an arrogant aristocracy never was spared.

The landed class "know something of agriculture—country members have to get it up for agricultural dinners—and they know something of horses—*and they know all that can be known on the subject of game.*"

The Peers are his favourite aversion, as a class that have monopolized land and a class that have usurped legislative power. He warned the people whom he addressed that "no law can pass, not the smallest modicum of freedom or of justice come to you, *until it has gone through the very fine meshes of the net of the House of Lords.*" On Privilege he wages a mortal warfare. The question between the Peers and the people, he declared in 1858, was one which could not be evaded. They were the great difficulty in the way of Reform. "Since 1690," he said, "when the Peers became the dominant power in this country, I am scarcely able to discover one single measure important to human or English freedom which has come from the voluntary consent and good will of their House. And really, how should it?" And then follows a portrait of the Peer drawn with a free hand:

"You know what a Peer is. He is one of those fortunate individuals who are described as coming into the world 'with a silver spoon in their mouths.' Or, to use the more polished and elaborate phraseology of the poet, it may be said of him —

> " ' Fortune came smiling to his youth and wooed it,
> And purpled greatness met his ripened years.'

"When he is a boy, among his brothers and sisters, he is pre-eminent; he is the eldest son; he will be my Lord; this beautiful park, these countless farms, this vast political influence, will one day centre on this innocent boy. The servants know it, and pay him greater deference on account of it. He grows up and goes to school and college; his future position is known; he has no great incitement to work hard, because, whatever he does, it is very difficult for him to improve his fortune in any way. When he leaves college, he has a position ready-made for him, and there seems to be no reason why he should follow ardently any of those occupations which make men great among their fellow-men. He takes his seat in the House of Peers; whatever may be his character, whatever his intellect, whatever his previous life, whether he be in England or 10,000 miles away, be he tottering down the steep of age, or be he passing through the imbecility of second childhood: yet, by means of that charming contrivance—made only for Peers—vote by proxy, he gives his vote for or against, and unfortunately too often against, all those great measures on which you and the country have set their hearts."

If possible, he likes the Bishops still less, and no sentence he ever uttered gave greater offence than his description of these prelates :—" There is another kind of Peer which I am afraid to touch upon, that creature of—what shall I say?—of monstrous, nay, even of adulterous birth—the spiritual peer."

Seven speeches on America are given. We do not need to consult them in order to know Mr. Bright's opinion on the war. Of the few steady friends whom we had in England during the Rebellion, Mr. Bright was the foremost. Few of us will ever know how much it cost a public man in England to be a friend to America from 1861 to 1865 and 1866. He put at stake his popularity, his leadership—nay, his political existence. If he had any reputation for sagacity, he risked it all by believing it possible that the Union should survive. He could not meet his friends in the street, he could not accept an invitation to dinner, without exposing himself to insult. At no time was the hatred against America more furious than when news came of the *Trent* seizure. A timid man might have held his peace till that storm blew over. Mr. Bright chose the moment when the hurricane was at its height to deliver an address at a public banquet given him by his townsmen of Rochdale. It is marked by great moderation of statement, and equally marked by the most clear presentation of the cause of the North, of the sins of the South, and of the duty of England. He rebuked Lord John Russell for the utterance of that memorable epigram : "The North is contending for empire, the South for independence." He dared to say of the *Times*, which at that moment was clamouring for war, that it had not published, since Mr. Lincoln took office, one fair and honourable and friendly article on American affairs. He had observed, also, the course of some American papers, which had been the strongest partisans of the South, but which, when the war broke out, were compelled by regard for their own safety to turn round and appear to take the other side. But they undertook to serve the South in another way, by kindling a quarrel with England. "If," said Mr. Bright, "the *Times* has done all it could to poison the minds of the people of England, the *New York Herald* has equally done all it could, or all it dared, to provoke mischief between the two countries." He invoked a fair and dispassionate consideration of the *Trent* dispute. How many other voices were heard at that moment in England in such an appeal? And he uttered a prayer destined not to be granted, for it depended on others, accompanied by a pledge which has been fulfilled to the letter, for it depended on himself alone. The speech concludes :—

" Now whether the Union will be restored or not, or the South achieve an unhonoured independence or not, I know not and I predict not. But this I think I know—that in a few years, a very few years, the twenty millions of freemen in the North will be thirty millions, or even fifty millions—a population equal to or exceeding that of this kingdom. When that time comes, I pray that it may not be said amongst them that in the darkest hour of their country's trials, England, the land of their fathers, looked on with icy coldness and saw unmoved the perils and calamities of their children. As for me, I have but this to say : I am but one in this audience, and but one in the citizenship of this country ; but if all other tongues are silent, mine shall speak for that policy which gives hope to the bondsmen of the South, and which tends to generous thoughts, and generous words, and generous deeds, between the two great nations who speak the English language, and from their origin are alike entitled to the English name."

All the speeches on America abound in examples of eloquence that Americans will delight to read, and they are a record of such good will to America, and such clear views of the policy that England ought to have pursued, and did not, as most British statesmen may now peruse with envy and regret. It is well understood that Mr. Bright is to take office in the next Liberal Government. Heretofore he has been a minister without a portfolio, discharging those functions which no Cabinet Minister burdened with

official responsibilities can execute, the representa-
tive of the great body of the people of England
otherwise unrepresented in Parliament, creating the
opinion which made a Liberal Government to some
extent possible. He abdicates the higher office to
assume the lower. Probably he is not of that opinion
— few men in England will be. Possession of
office is the evidence of political respectability, and
it will be deemed fitting that as the period of this
momentous change approaches, the record of his
past career should be brought before the world. He
has been many things to many men. Go back three
years, and ask the first ten hurrying pedestrians you
meet in the Strand, who is John Bright ? An agitator,
a demagogue, a revolutionist, disloyal to the Crown,
eager to overthrow the House of Lords, reviler of the
Church and the Bishops, a Socialist, an Agrarian, very
likely an infidel. Possibly the tenth man might
answer, a loyal, religious, gifted statesman and orator,
one of few men in this kingdom who clearly understands its history, its condition, and its necessities,
and, understanding, has the genius and courage to
attempt a reform. But to him, as he himself said
of a man greatly his inferior, "it has been given in
a manner not often permitted to those who do great

things of this kind, to see the ripe fruit of his vast labours."

Johnson said that Fox had divided the kingdom with Cæsar; so that it was a doubt whether the nation should be ruled by the sceptre of George the Third or the tongue of Fox. In those days the comparison was a striking one, for George the Third controlled by his personal will the policy of the Empire. Now the sceptre of Victoria is a shadow, the House of Commons is King, and its legislation follows the voice of its greatest orator.

THE END.

R. CLAY, SONS, AND TAYLOR, PRINTERS, BREAD STREET HILL.

www.ingramcontent.com/pod-product-compliance
Lightning Source LLC
Chambersburg PA
CBHW031931060726
47496CB00008BA/2864